Make it Snappy, Elephant

For Kevin

W.

ORCHARD BOOKS
96 Leonard Street, London EC2A 4RH
Orchard Books Australia
14 Mars Road, Lane Cove, NSW 2066
First published in Great Britain 1996
First paperback publication 1997
Text © Pat Moon 1996
Illustrations © Woody 1996
The right of Pat Moon to be identified as the Author
and Woody as the Illustrator of this Work
has been asserted by them in accordance with the
Copyright, Designs and Patents Act, 1988.
A CIP catalogue record for this book is available
from the British Library.
1 86039 192 3 (hardback)
1 86039 238 5 (paperback)
Printed in Great Britain

Make it
Snappy,
Elephant

Pat Moon

Illustrated by
Woody

 ORCHARD BOOKS

Turtle was taking his early
morning swim.

SNAP!
But just in time, Turtle dived.

Croc was really angry. But he wasn't showing it.

"Don't rush off, dear Turtle," he called. "I only want to say hello." And he grinned horribly.

"Where are you, dear Turtle?" he called softly.

"As far away from you as I can get!" yelled Turtle popping up his head.

Then Turtle dived again.

And Croc was thrashing after
him.
But Croc was clever.
He stopped thrashing.

He sank slowly-oh-so-slowly down, waiting for the mud to settle so he could see.
And there was Turtle, not so far away, paddling for the bank.

And oh-so-silently, under the water, Croc glided after him... just a bite away!

But Croc's jaws snapped onto
nothing but water...
as Turtle took off – safe in
Crane's beak.

"You stupid turtle!" said Crane
when they got back.
"You're asking for trouble –
cheeking that crocodile.
Lucky for you I was flying past.

Only a tooth away from being Croc's breakfast!"

"It takes more than some old croc to catch me," said Turtle.

But Crane, Cheetah, Chimp and Elephant couldn't help noticing how Turtle was shaking.

Each time Turtle went to the river, Croc was waiting.
"Do come in, dear Turtle," he sniggered.

He glided towards Turtle.

Then suddenly Croc sprang out, charging after Turtle along the bank.
Luckily for Turtle, Crane was just in time again.

17

"Hey, Croc," called Elephant.
"You leave Turtle alone, now.
Pick on someone your own size -
like me."

"I wouldn't dream of it. You're as tough as an old tree. No – it's that little Turtle I want. Have you ever tasted turtle, dear friend?"

"Never," said Elephant.

"Dee-licious! The tastiest bite-size snack," said Croc.

"Like a pie. Crisp and crunchy on the outside.
Soft and juicy on the inside.
Yum-yum.

Makes my mouth water just thinking about it."

Day after day, Croc lay waiting.
Turtle didn't dare go near the
river.

"It's no good!" yelled Turtle one day. "I'm going to the river! I need water!"

"Or Croc will get you. As sure as Cheetah's got spots," said Elephant.

Then Elephant dug out a big
hole with her tusks.

She sucked up water from the
river and filled that hole.
"There you are, Turtle.
Your own little swimming pool!"

Aaaaa! Thanks Elephant.

Next time Elephant was down at the river, Croc said,
"It looks as if that Turtle has you doing all the fetching and carrying, Elephant. Why put up with it, eh?"

And he grinned his horrible grin.

Each day Elephant filled Turtle's pool.

26

"Here - look what I've made,"
said Chimp who was playing
with the mud. "Guess who this
is."

"Well look – it's Elephant!" cried
Crane.

"Brilliant!" said Cheetah.

"And it's given me a brilliant
idea..." thought Elephant.

"I've been thinking, Croc," said Elephant next time she went to the river.

"Maybe you're right about Turtle. I'm tired of fetching and carrying."

"My dear friend," grinned Croc.
"Let me help.
You just tell that little Turtle that
I've gone away.
I'll hide behind those reeds down
river.

Then when he swims by ...
CRUNCH! Your little problem's
gone!"
He sniggered horribly.
"But make it snappy, Elephant!
My tummy's rumbling."

Let's say tomorrow morning – for BREAKFAST!

When Elephant got back she
said, "Chimp – look what I
found. This nice round stone.
I bet you can't use some of that
mud to make it look like Turtle."

"Bet I can," said Chimp and he set to work.

"Crane," said Elephant, "it's too hot. Could you weave me a big fan from those reeds there, so I can cool myself down?"

"Easy," said Crane.
"Thanks, Crane."

"Cheetah," said Elephant later. "What do you think of Chimp's turtle?"

"Really good!" said Cheetah. "Except for the eyes. Here, Chimp – use these tiny shiny

black pebbles."
"Perfect, Chimp," said Elephant.
"What do you think, Turtle?"
"What a handsome turtle!" said
Turtle.

Early next morning Elephant
fetched Crane's fan and Chimp's
turtle and woke everyone up.

She lead them to the bushes up river.

"It makes me feel nervy being so close to the river," shivered Turtle.

"Sshh! Relax, Turtle," whispered Elephant. "Now everyone, listen carefully. I'm off down river. When you hear me trumpet,

I want you to push this out."
She set down Crane's fan. And
she put Chimp's mud turtle on
top.
"Make sure it floats down river.
But stay out of sight," she
warned.

"Is someone going to tell me
what this is all about?"
grumbled Cheetah.
"You'll see," said Elephant.
"Just watch those reeds down
river."

"Pssss!" called Elephant to Croc,
who was waiting in the reeds.
"It's all fixed. Turtle's waiting for
me to trumpet.
Then he'll think it's safe to swim.

But he's quick and tricky, that
Turtle. You'd better snap him up
fast!"
Croc grinned.

It'll be a pleasure,
my dear Elephant.

Elephant trumpeted.

Crane pushed out the fan. It
floated off.
"Look!" said Chimp. "It's just
like the real Turtle!"

Croc was drooling and dribbling when he saw what was gliding towards him.

SPLASH!
Out jumped Croc.

SNAP! went his jaws on the turtle.

CRUNCH! CRACK! went his teeth as they bit the stone.

"YEOUW!!" spluttered Croc.

And Chimp, Cheetah, Crane
and Turtle jumped and cheered.
"Good old Elephant!"

"I think you're going to be sucking worms for a bit, Croc," laughed Cheetah.
"Now you just clear off! You hear, Croc?" yelled Elephant.
"And make it snappy!"

And Croc cleared off.